Incredibly
Disgusting
Drugs

Downers:
Depressant Abuse

Jason Porterfield

rosen publishing's
**rosen
central**

New York

Published in 2008 by The Rosen Publishing Group, Inc.
29 East 21st Street, New York, NY 10010

Copyright © 2008 by The Rosen Publishing Group, Inc.

First Edition

Library of Congress Cataloging-in-Publication Data

Porterfield, Jason.
Downers: depressant abuse / Jason Porterfield. — 1st ed.
      p. cm. — (Incredibly disgusting drugs)
Includes bibliographical references and index.
ISBN-13: 978-1-4042-1957-1 (library binding)
ISBN-10: 1-4042-1957-9 (library binding)
1. Central nervous system depressants—Juvenile literature. 2. Hypnotics—Juvenile literature. 3. Sedatives—Juvenile literature. 4. Tranquilizing drugs—Juvenile literature. I. Title.
RM330.P67 2008
615'.782—dc22

                                                    2007005437

Manufactured in China

Contents

Introduction

owners, or depressants, are among the oldest known drugs. Depressants are drugs that slow the activity of the central nervous system. These drugs have existed in the forms of opium and alcohol for thousands of years. More recently, downers have been manufactured in laboratories—first as barbiturates and later as drugs known as benzodiazepines. They've been prescribed and sold as sedatives, painkillers, and other kinds of drugs that prevent seizures and convulsions. At times, they've been called wonder drugs. Today, researchers continue to make new forms of benzodiazepines.

However, even the potentially most useful drugs have a downside. Barbiturates were found to be highly addictive and were actually proven deadly. Benzodiazepines are far less dangerous, but the potential for harm remains.

Despite the fact that many benzodiazepines are manufactured and sold legally for medical usage in the United States, using and abusing them on your own is not legal. Apart from issues with the law, a person abusing these drugs runs the risk of falling into a dangerous spiral of addiction. Yes, the addict is using a drug that is legal under certain circumstances, but the drug itself is still addictive. Worse, a tolerance for the drug could build up, causing the abuser to turn to harder, more dangerous drugs—after all, the illegal and highly dangerous drug heroin is also a downer. The addict's life will likely fall apart, leaving recovery or a further fall into addiction as his or her only options.

Once the addict recognizes the problem, he or she can start on the long road to recovery. Lucky addicts may not have to face jail time, disease, or permanent physical and/or psychological damage. However, few addicts are that fortunate. With treatment and support, they may be able to rebuild their lives. Let's take a closer look at the incredibly disgusting and addictive drugs that are called downers.

1

An Incredibly
Disgusting Problem

recent report issued by the University of Michigan stated that drug use by eighth, tenth, and twelfth graders has dropped sharply—by 23 percent—since 2001. Not all of the news is good, however. Use of prescription drugs by teens has increased, particularly among those who abuse the prescription painkiller OxyContin and sedatives; the number of teens abusing the prescription painkiller Vicodin remained the same. These sedatives and painkillers are often referred to as downers, which is a broad category of illegal or controlled drugs that includes substances that depress the central nervous system.

The U.S. government classifies more than 178 drugs as illegal. These illegal drugs include really disgusting and highly addictive substances such as cocaine, heroin, and methamphetamine, as well as others that aren't as popular. All are considered potentially harmful to users. Even drugs that aren't

Teresa Ashcraft speaks with Florida's then attorney general Charlie Crist in 2004 as an advocate for increased oversight of prescription drugs. Her son died of an OxyContin overdose.

abused all that much, such as the hallucinogen peyote, are classified as illegal.

Many legal drugs can do gross things to the body. They remain legal because they have other uses besides intoxication that far outweigh the danger of their abuse. Chemicals such as gasoline, glue, and cleaning products that can be inhaled to produce a high fall into this category. Many legal drugs, especially painkillers and sleeping aids, have a high potential for abuse. Therefore, they can be purchased only with a doctor's prescription.

Getting High on Downers

People use downers for a number of different reasons, none of them good. They may experiment with these drugs because they think that it'll be fun, or because their friends are doing it. Like many other risky behaviors, trying downers can seem like a way for a person to prove that he or she is cool and unafraid of the damage these substances can cause.

When experimenting with downers, people may forget about the dangers of these drugs. For example, they may overdose or experience a seizure, neither of which are fun. Their judgment may be impaired, leading them to make poor decisions or to do something that puts them in harm's way. They may get caught with the drug and be thrown in jail. Worse, they may die, possibly after trying downers for the first time.

That's not all, though. Downers may negatively affect learning abilities or damage the brain. Long-term abuse negatively affects vital organs such as the heart, making users more susceptible to disease. In the end, downers may consume a person's life, causing him or her to destroy old relationships and to lose everything.

What Exactly Are Downers?

Illegal drugs are commonly classified into four categories: hallucinogens, stimulants (uppers), opiates/opioids, and depressants (downers). Hallucinogens, sometimes referred to as psychedelics or psychomimetics, alter a person's perceptions and include such drugs as LSD, PCP, and marijuana. Stimulants such as cocaine and amphetamines excite the central nervous system, making you highly alert and overly stimulated. Opiates and opioids slow the nervous system and cause feelings of great pleasure, or euphoria. Opiates, including heroin and morphine, are naturally derived from opium. Opioids are synthetically produced, or man-made, drugs that mimic the effects of opiates.

Downers are drugs that inhibit the central nervous system. These drugs include sedatives, which relax the body, and hypnotics, which induce sleep. Because they slow the central nervous system, opiates, opioids, and alcohol are considered downers as well.

There are many drugs that are considered downers, from legal alcoholic beverages to the illegal and highly disgusting opioid heroin. Alcohol has been consumed for thousands of years and was the main ingredient in many medicines sold in the United States before the twentieth century. Opiates have been in use as painkillers for thousands of years, while opioids have been around since the nineteenth century.

In its purified form, heroin is a fine white powder. This variety, called "black tar" heroin, is commonly produced in mobile labs in Mexico.

A man tries unsuccessfully to walk a straight line in a sobriety test after being stopped at a checkpoint for driving under the influence of alcohol.

Medically prescribed doses of downers have few noticeable effects on a person's basic physical abilities. However, the ability of the user to do somewhat basic tasks, such as following street directions or driving, can become seriously impaired.

All forms of downers, from alcohol to phenobarbital, make users feel as if they are escaping from their daily lives. They feel like they are able to calm down when their lives seemingly spiral out of control. The sad irony is that an addiction to downers only makes one's problems worse. Rather than focusing on solving their problems by getting the proper help, drug users find that their dependence on downers increases until addiction consumes their life.

The
Different Types
of Downers

here are many types of downers, but they all do pretty much the same disgusting things to the body. At first, the user becomes relaxed. This feeling gives way to general mellowness. Higher doses may bring on light-headedness as well as drowsiness. Learning, memory, and coordination may be impaired. Depending on the strength of the depressant, these effects could last anywhere from a couple hours to more than a day.

Barbiturates, benzodiazepine-based tranquilizers, and gamma hydroxybutyrate (GHB) are the drugs that are most commonly considered downers. Barbiturates and benzodiazepines include pills that are taken as sedatives, sleep aids, anesthetics, and anticonvulsants. GHB commonly comes in the form of an odorless and colorless liquid.

The effects of barbiturate and benzodiazepine use are similar to those of alcohol. A person who has been

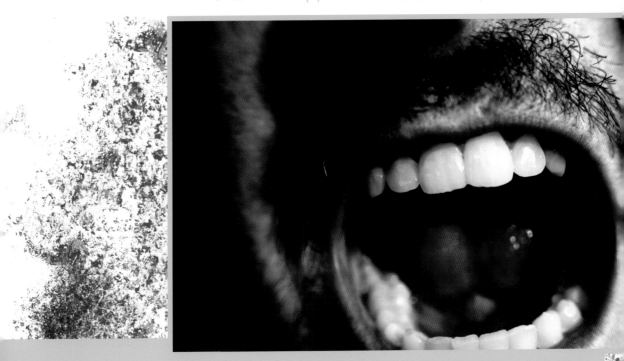

Although downers generally produce feelings of relaxation, abuse can trigger side effects such as anxiety, aggression, and rage.

taking barbiturates may slur his or her speech, act disoriented, and become more sociable, doing things that he or she would never do under better judgment.

High doses of barbiturates can bring on intense mood swings and aggressive behavior. The user may walk unsteadily and lose his or her muscle coordination. Learning and memory are impaired, as is judgment. Extremely elevated doses of barbiturates or doses mixed with other drugs can result in coma or even death. Other disgusting side effects include anxiety, rage, and nightmares. The effects of all depressants are intensified by alcohol.

Barbiturates

German pharmacists first discovered barbiturates in 1864. These drugs were derived from barbituric acid. The first barbiturate to be marketed to the public was a sleeping pill called barbital, which was introduced in 1903. Other early barbiturates were used to treat nervous disorders such as anxiety. Doctors considered them effective and safe, though they've been available only with a prescription since the 1930s.

At their peak in the 1950s, barbiturates were manufactured in about 50 varieties. Some were marketed for human consumption, and many others were sold for use on animals. The most popular were Dolophine (also known as methadone) and Seconal. The drugs gained prominence as a number of Hollywood stars and other high-profile entertainers used them.

Even though barbiturates can help with sicknesses, the amount needed to cure any ailments is dangerous. During the 1960s, many people who had been prescribed barbiturates over a long period of time had become addicted to them. Overdoses were common, and mixing the drugs with alcohol often proved deadly.

At one point, approximately 3,000 people a year died from taking barbiturates, and about half of them were suicides. Celebrity deaths linked to barbiturates include Marilyn Monroe and Elvis Presley. Today,

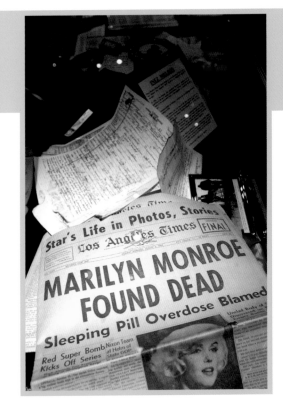

The legendary actress Marilyn Monroe died in 1962, at the age of thirty-six, after an overdose of the prescription barbiturate Nembutal.

there are only about a dozen different kinds of barbiturates available.

There are three main types of barbiturates: long-acting barbiturates, intermediate or short-acting barbiturates, and very short-acting barbiturates. Long-acting barbiturates have effects that last from twelve to twenty-four hours. These drugs are most often prescribed to treat seizures and mild anxiety. Common long-acting barbiturates include barbital, phenobarbital, mephobarbital, and theophylline.

Intermediate or short-acting barbiturates have effects that typically last from six to seven hours, and their impact is similar to that of alcohol. In small doses, they may cause a general sensation of mild excitement. Moderate doses provide a pleasant sense of well-being, while higher doses can produce heavy, stuporlike conditions that are comparable to

When someone passes around barbiturates or other downers, there's the chance that what was supposed to be a fun night could lead to overdose and death.

extreme drunkenness. Traditionally, these drugs were prescribed for short-term treatment of insomnia and were used to sedate patients prior to undergoing an operation. The barbiturates pentobarbital, secobarbital, butalbital, butabarbital, talbutal, and aprobarbital all fall into this category.

Very short-acting barbiturates take effect within minutes and can make you unconscious almost immediately. They are generally injected and used as anesthesia. Very short-acting barbiturates include methohexital, thiamylal, and thiopental. High doses of any barbiturates depress important brain functions, particularly that which controls breathing.

Over time, an assortment of funny nicknames has been concocted for barbiturates. Generally, barbiturates have been called "dolls" or "dollies." Many of the street names for individual barbiturates refer to how the pills look, or they are shortened versions of the name. Pentobarbital pills are sometimes called "nebbies," "yellow jackets," or just "yellows." Phenobarbital pills are often called "purple hearts," while amobarbital pills are called "blues" and secobarbital pills go under the name of "reds," "red devils," or "red birds."

Though barbiturates are nowhere near as common today as they were fifty years ago, about 4 percent of the U.S. population has taken some form of barbiturate for a nonmedical reason. People take them either to bring themselves down after taking amphetamines or to increase the high from using heroin.

With barbiturates, abuse often equals death. The wide range of effects induced by these drugs when properly prescribed covers everything from mild sedation to inducing comas. Users accustomed to taking one barbiturate and who know how much they need to induce a certain feeling may decide to experiment with a drug with a similar-sounding name if their substance of choice is unavailable. This is a mistake that could prove fatal. For example, the number of phenobarbital pills that would make up a "safe" dose would prove fatal if pentobarbital were used instead. There's a subtle difference in spelling but a severe difference in substance when it comes to the two drugs. There's also the possibility that a user may simply forget how many pills he or she has already ingested. As a result, the user may take more, going beyond the safe threshold.

Benzodiazepines

Benzodiazepine—a chemical derived from *Rauwolfia serpentina*, a bush native to Africa and Asia—is commonly used in folk remedies. Chemists discovered it in the 1950s; they were looking for a safer alternative to barbiturates. Benzodiazepines have many of the same properties as the earlier barbiturates, but without some of the disgusting side effects. Unlike barbiturates, benzodiazepines can be effective as a medicine in small amounts. Therefore, they are far less likely to cause a fatal overdose unless they are used with other drugs.

Benzodiazepines are much safer than barbiturates because they don't affect a person's breathing, as barbiturates can. However, they can make the user drowsy and uncoordinated, and can impair his or her learning and short-term memory.

When the first benzodiazepine (chlordiazepoxide, or Librium) was made in 1957, it was seen as a major medical breakthrough, even though researchers couldn't say for certain how the drug worked.

When properly used, benzodiazepines can greatly reduce anxiety. In addition, users are less likely to have an overdose, as long as the drugs are not used in tandem with another type of downer. There are only a few known cases of fatal overdoses involving benzodiazepines. In most of those cases, the person had used them with alcohol or some other drug.

Though far safer than barbiturates, benzodiazepines do have drawbacks. They can make the user sleepy and uncoordinated, which can have dangerous consequences if he or she decides to drive a car or

A driver under the influence of downers is a danger to himself and to others, since the drugs cause disorientation and impaired coordination.

operate other equipment, such as power tools. Other common side effects include lightheadedness, dizziness, lack of coordination, and nightmares. The drugs can also seriously affect the ability to learn and can sometimes cause amnesia, as the drug fools around with a person's brain functions.

Users do develop a tolerance to benzodiazepines. This causes them to use the drug more and more. They must also suffer through an extended withdrawal period while trying to kick the habit. Once the user stops taking benzodiazepines, problems with learning often go away.

One of the most controversial aspects of benzodiazepine use involves the way in which the drugs hurt your memory. The drugs can affect both long-term and short-term memory and cause amnesia. Some benzodiazepines, particularly flunitrazepam (sold under the brand name Rohypnol; pills are often called "roofies"), have developed a reputation as "date rape drugs" because they can be easily slipped into a person's drink. The unsuspecting victim may have no memory of events that occur under the influence of the drug, even sexual assault.

Since the discovery of benzodiazepines, there have been more than 3,000 types made. Perhaps the most famous is the tranquilizer Valium. Other well-known examples of benzodiazepines include Xanax, Librium, and Halcion.

Gamma Hydroxybutyrate

Gamma hydroxybutyrate (GHB) is used as a general anesthetic in many European countries. In the United States, it has been sold in health-food stores as a bodybuilding aide, but it was banned for over-the-counter sales by the U.S. Food and Drug Administration in 1990. It is, however, still available by prescription under the name Xyrem, and it is used to treat the sleep disorder narcolepsy. Illegally obtained GHB is most commonly found at parties and all-night raves. The drug is easy to make, difficult to detect if disguised in a drink, and extremely dangerous.

GHB is both a man-made drug and a naturally occurring substance found in the central nervous systems of human beings. It was first made in 1960 by a French researcher named Dr. Henri Laborit, who had hoped to discover a new anesthetic. While the drug did put patients in deep comas, it did not prevent pain.

A by-product of fermentation, trace amounts of GHB are occasionally found in some wines and beers. Almost always ingested as a liquid, GHB can easily cross from the bloodstream to the central nervous system and the brain itself. Scientists are still unsure of what GHB's role in the brain might be, but they believe that increasing the amount already there activates parts of the brain at random.

GHB produces temporary sensations of relaxation and mild euphoria that can lead to side effects such as dizziness, headaches, nausea, and even seizures and death. Today, GHB is only legal in the United States as Xyrem. All other uses have been made illegal.

Alcohol

Alcohol has a long history of being used as a depressant. Alcohol is legal in the United States, though its sale is regulated by laws on the local, state, and national levels. It is also federally taxed. Today, the age at which it is legal to drink alcohol anywhere in the United States is twenty-one.

Alcohol is produced in one of two ways: fermentation or distillation. Fermented beverages such as beer or wine generally have a lower alcohol content than distilled liquors, like whiskey and vodka. The effects of alcohol on an individual depend on a number of factors, including body weight and whether he or she has acquired a tolerance for alcohol. The type of beverage consumed, the rate at which it is consumed, and whether

Long-term alcohol abuse can lead to cirrhosis, or hardening, of the liver, a condition that is irreversible and often leads to liver failure.

the individual has eaten recently are all factors in how drinking will impact a person.

The effects of alcohol on the body are well documented. Alcohol can impair memory, coordination, judgment, reflexes, and motor skills. In excessive amounts, it can cause illness, including liver and heart problems, or death. Chronic use can result in addiction, which is referred to as alcoholism.

Opiates and Opioids

Opiates and opioids are among the most dangerous downers. They are highly addictive. Opium, the best-known opiate, is extracted from the opium poppy. It is then either smoked in the form of a resin or consumed in a liquid extract such as laudanum.

Opioids include synthetically produced morphine and heroin, both of which were originally manufactured to replicate opium's painkilling effects without its addictive qualities. However, both drugs proved to be highly addictive.

3

The **Ugly** Truth

eople who experiment with drugs don't typically set out to become addicted. They might try drugs out of curiosity, to fit in, or to escape from boredom or depression. Drug use becomes abuse when it begins creeping into other aspects of a person's life, causing problems.

The Dangers of Abuse

All downers—legal and illegal—affect the body's central nervous system in one way or another. In the case of legal downers, recommended guidelines can be set forth on the packaging of over-the-counter tablets designed to cure a headache or flu symptoms. Doctors recommend dosages for prescription medications, and the prescription instructs pharmacists as to how much of a certain drug should be distributed at once, while limiting the number of times the prescription can be filled. While there are no guidelines in circulation for how much alcohol should be consumed at once, federal law

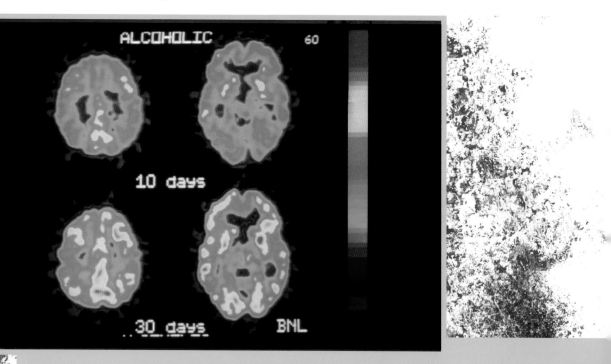

The effects of alcohol abstinence are revealed on this scan of the brain. The brighter yellow areas, representing higher brain activity, increase after a longer period of sobriety.

forbids people under the age of twenty-one from purchasing, possessing, or using alcohol at all.

How downers affect an individual could depend on many factors. A person's age and gender are important to consider. People's brains continue to develop through their teenage years and into their early twenties. Downer abuse during those years can seriously impair brain development. For many people, the first social experiences with downers eventually turn into a drug habit. As an example, about half of all adults in the United States occasionally drink alcohol. Of those, about 10 percent drink heavily. Approximately 5 percent follow addictive drinking patterns.

A person's metabolism can be another factor. Downers can stay in some people's systems for longer periods of time. A person's physical condition—whether he or she is in shape or has been ill—also can have an impact on the effects of downers. Someone who's been ill or has a preexisting medical condition may be more susceptible to a downer drug and therefore be more prone to a fatal overdose. A previously unknown allergy could cause serious medical problems if activated by downers.

With illegal downers, there is the added risk of not being able to count on a drug's purity, or strength, or whether the drug is actually what the dealer claims it is. Illegal drug manufacturers and dealers "cut" drugs before distributing them to users, meaning that the downer is mixed with something that decreases its purity and increases its volume so they can make more money. If someone uses a downer that is significantly purer than what he or she is used to, an overdose can occur. In contrast, some-one using a downer that's weaker than what he or she is accustomed to may try to compensate with other drugs, with results that could be fatal.

From 2005 to 2006, heroin that had been cut with the powerful opioid fentanyl began appearing on the streets of many Midwestern cities. Fentanyl, which is a tightly controlled medical drug, is hundreds of times more powerful than heroin, and many unsuspecting heroin users died after injecting the drug.

An Ugly Lifestyle

Other consequences affect the lives of those around a user. Drugs alter the way the body works. With downers, loss of judgment and motor control are two of the usual side effects. If a person using downers decides to drive somewhere, the consequences can be deadly. With the exception of alcohol, there's no detectable odor for downers, so a person's friends might not realize that he or she has taken the drugs. There's also no way to know how many downers a person has taken, or what kind.

As a person's drug use grows out of control, his or her life will quickly start to unravel. A habitual drug user may start missing school or work, instead choosing to get high or to sleep off the effects of the previous night's binge. As the use of downers deepens, more of the user's income goes toward buying the drugs, while less is spent on necessities such as groceries or paying bills.

The user's appearance starts slipping, as well as the appearance of his or her home as minor details like cleanliness stop seeming important. Too many unexcused absences and a deteriorating performance at work may cause the user to get fired. Debts start piling up, and the user is forced to start selling off possessions in order to fund the increasingly expensive drug habit. The user may even start committing crimes to get the money needed to get high.

As dependence on downers increases, users may not care how they take them. Those who once smoked a downer, for example, may find that method no longer delivers the drug into the bloodstream quickly

Downer abuse and homelessness often go hand in hand, especially among young adults. A homeless youth living on the street typically has a life expectancy of only twenty-six years.

enough. They may begin injecting it with a needle instead. With intravenous injection, the chance of users contracting HIV or another blood-based disease through a contaminated needle goes up, as does the risk of contracting an infection through needle use, dying from injecting an air bubble, and dying from an overdose, as injected drugs enter the blood-stream far faster than drugs taken through other methods. Permanent damage to a person's health becomes a real possibility, as heavy drug

Drugs injected intravenously have almost an instantaneous effect. An overdose can have fatal results before the user can seek medical attention.

use wears on the brain, heart, and other vital organs.

Overdose!

Every drug user's nightmare is the overdose, the point at which the dose the user thought was safe is really too much. Overdoses can occur with any drug. It's even possible to overdose on caffeine! With downers, an overdose victim's breathing is suppressed and he or she can easily slip into a coma. Early signs of an overdose include extreme disorientation, loss of motor control, and sudden mood swings. The victim must be taken to a hospital right away, where the medical staff will try to identify the drug taken and get it out of the person's body by pumping out the contents of the stomach and inducing vomiting. Then they administer drugs to counteract the effects of the drug used, making it extremely vital that they know what sort of drug caused the overdose.

A barbiturate overdose resembles a person going into shock. The victim has cold and sweaty skin; has a fast, weak pulse; and breathes rapidly and shallowly. He or she may fall into a deep coma, or the kidneys or lungs may stop working. Barbiturates work by reducing the amount of oxygen that reaches the brain, so an overdose could result in permanent brain damage.

Cycle of Addiction

Addiction is the need to use a drug despite knowing that it's bad for you. Downers activate circuits within an individual's brain that respond to pleasure. Addiction occurs when a person's brain becomes accustomed to the pleasurable effects of downers to the extent that it needs them to feel as though it's functioning properly. A tolerance develops when previous amounts of a drug no longer bring on the pleasurable effects, meaning that the user must take larger doses of the drug.

Every person's brain has pleasure receptors, so everyone on the planet could potentially become addicted to downers. However, the tendency to become addicted seems to have some basis in genetics, meaning that some people are born with a greater predisposition to addiction than others.

There are four recognized steps toward downer addiction: experimental use, recreational use, instrumental use, and compulsive use. Experimental use is usually the short-term and random use of one or more substances, mainly out of curiosity or a desire to reach an altered state of mind. Recreational use is when people get together occasionally to take the drug.

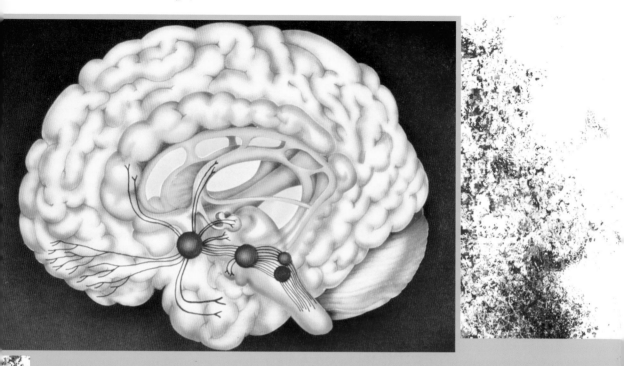

Heroin and other opiates work by binding to specific receptors in the brain, shown here in red. These sites help control pain, mood, and some physical functions of the body.

Instrumental use is the point at which the user starts taking downers for a specific purpose, either for pleasure or to combat unpleasant feelings such as guilt, shame, boredom, depression, stress, or loneliness. The user starts to change, and initial signs of dependence might start appearing. The user may drift away from old friends, spending more time alone or with people who also share an interest in the drug. The user's main form of recreation becomes getting high. A tolerance for downers forms, leading to heavier use. The person may experience mood swings and may no longer feel normal with or without the drug in his or her system.

Compulsive use is addiction, where the user's life is completely dominated by getting and using downers and forgetting about everything else. At this stage, the addict needs the drug to function properly and may become uncontrollable if the drug is cut off. The user will do anything to get the drug, even break the law. The addict will become paranoid and start hiding downers, even from friends. Most addicts don't recognize that they are addicted.

Abusing either legal or illegal downers can have serious consequences and can destroy a person's life and the lives of others. Repeated abuse can result in addiction, but even using downers just once can change a person's life for the worse forever.

Making
the Right
Choice

owner abuse can damage a person's finances, health, and mental stability. Friends and family may be harmed by an addict's habit, taken advantage of or used until they can no longer trust the person they thought they knew. In a worst-case scenario, the addict may physically harm someone through downer abuse.

All of these consequences are serious, but the effects of illegal downer use hurt all of society, as the people who sell drugs battle each other for territory, pollute with dangerous chemicals they use to produce and cut drugs, and keep police forces from focusing on other problems. The U.S. government spends millions of tax dollars each year fighting illegal drug trafficking. Without drug traffickers, the money could be spent somewhere else.

A Life Derailed

Possession of barbiturates, benzodiazepines, and GHB without a prescription is against the law. Underage

Rampant drug abuse and trafficking can transform friendly neighborhoods into crime-ridden slums. Here, police detain suspected drug offenders in New York City.

possession of alcohol is also illegal. Driving under the influence of drugs or alcohol is a serious offense. Possession of most opiates under any circumstance can get you thrown in jail.

Drug crimes are serious, with mandatory jail time for drug offenders depending on circumstances and the amount of the drug found in a person's possession. For offenders under the age of eighteen, a drug offense will likely land the person in juvenile court and result in mandatory counseling.

Abusing downers usually leads to prison. Many inmates, such as this one at the Sheridan Correctional Center in Sheridan, Illinois, are locked up for drug and alcohol abuse.

The person could possibly end up in a juvenile home. The offense may go on the person's permanent record, meaning it will not be forgotten, and could follow the individual for the rest of his or her life.

As of 2000, about 21 percent of the national prison population serving time in state institutions was there because of drug offenses. As of 2003, approximately 55 percent of the 158,426 inmates in federal prisons were convicted of drug crimes. Many of those offenders started experimenting with downers at an early age.

Even if a user of downers avoids jail, he or she must still deal with recovery. After the addict quits using downers and is considered recovered, he or she must somehow return to daily life. That life will probably be very different than life before drugs. Returning to school could be difficult, as a former addict must make up weeks or months of lessons and may fail many classes. For someone in high school, this kind of discouragement may lead the person to drop out entirely without ever earning a diploma. Dropping out can seriously harm a person's chances of finding a good job or completing his or her education.

The recovered addict must get back to family and friends. People who have been seriously hurt or taken advantage of because of the person's addiction may not want to forgive. Even family members willing to forgive may not treat a former addict the same. They may always seem to be keeping an eye on him or her. Friends connected with drug use should have no place in a former addict's life.

Downers and Society

Downers come from everywhere. Including barbiturates and benzodiazepines, they are mainly gotten from prescription users. They're either stolen or acquired by dealers through fraud. This makes stopping their abuse extremely difficult.

The United States budgets about $40 billion a year to fight the war on drugs, covering everything from equipment for law enforcement to education initiatives. Other costs, however, do not factor into this budget. Worker productivity lost due to downers and other drug abuse is not accounted for. The loss of businesses in communities where drug dealers and users have taken over the streets is not counted either. Communities must also deal with the cost of cleaning up areas where drug manufacturers have damaged the environment by dumping chemicals. Unless drugs can be eliminated by law enforcement, treatment will need to continue.

Recognizing the Problem

Even when a user has recognized his or her dependence on downers, the habit is extremely hard to break. By the time the realization hits, the user's health may be impaired and his or her life may be in tatters. If the user is lucky, he or she will have friends and family who are willing to assist on the road to recovery, lending help and support throughout the process of kicking downers.

When a user stops taking the drug, withdrawal occurs. Withdrawal is the body's reaction to not getting the drugs it has become accustomed to. The effects of withdrawal depend on the type of downers the addict uses. Withdrawal from barbiturates can cause a wide variety of symptoms, like irritability, nervousness, fatigue, nausea, weakness, loss of appetite, fever, headache, muscleaches, and insomnia. Withdrawal may also cause disorientation. Abruptly quitting a severe addiction could bring on delirium and cause the victim to have convulsions or go into shock. Unlike most other drugs, withdrawal from barbiturates can actually kill you. The aftereffects of withdrawal from other downers are much the same, but without the possibility of death that comes with using barbiturates.

Withdrawal from downers can be physically and psychologically excruciating. At rehabilitation clinics, addicts are given medication to gradually ease them out of their addiction.

Getting Treatment

Withdrawal from downers should not be done alone. That is especially true of withdrawal from barbiturates. The addict should enroll in a medically supervised treatment program. Treatment programs are either inpatient or outpatient. Inpatient programs require the person undergoing treatment to stay in a hospital or group home where he or she can be monitored. Many court-ordered treatments are inpatient. In outpatient programs, the patient is allowed to stay off of hospital grounds but must come in for therapy sessions.

Treatment follows a process in which the recovering addict is educated about the dangers of the drug that he or she is trying to give up, as well as the hazards of addiction itself. The recovering addict will probably meet individually with a therapist to discuss any problems with recovery and to receive counseling on how to put his or her life back together. He or she will likely attend group therapy sessions, which are meetings in which addicts—likely people addicted to the same substance—gather in the presence of a counselor to talk about their addiction and recovery. The idea behind group therapy is that members will feel comfortable sharing with people in the same situation and they are likelier to lend support to those going through the same experience.

Generally, recovery from drug addiction occurs in six stages: pre-contemplation, contemplation, preparation, action, maintenance, and termination. These stages range from thinking about the problem and accepting it to finally acting to end it.

Before addicts can recover from the disgusting effects of drug addiction, they must recognize that they have a drug problem in the first place. This happens during the pre-contemplation stage, when addicts are still in denial. Addicts typically deny that they have a problem, or they place the blame outside of themselves, instead blaming their family, society, or even their genetic makeup.

Once addicts acknowledge that they have a drug problem, they enter the contemplation stage. Users make a plan to change their behavior

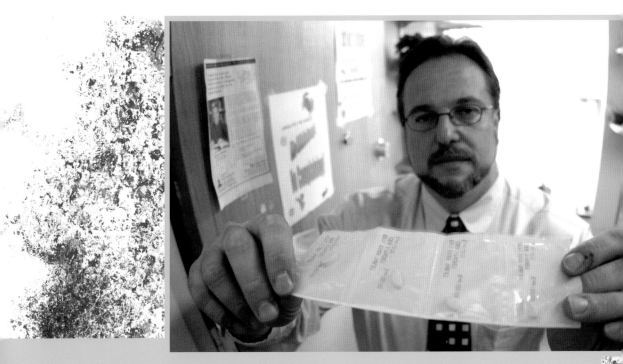

Experts are constantly investigating improved methods of treating drug addiction. Above, Dr. Warren Bickel leads clinical trials of buprenorphine, a new opiate withdrawal drug.

within a set time frame, often within six months, complete with a set of strategies designed to help them cope with withdrawal. Addicts at this stage are still focused on their past problems and not on the future, meaning that true change may still be years off.

At the preparation stage, addicts begin to take actual steps toward changing their behavior by setting a date to begin the change. The action stage is the abrupt behavioral change itself, and it will likely call for a major commitment of time and energy, as well as unwavering support from others.

At the maintenance stage, the goal has been achieved but addicts have to remain focused on avoiding behavior that could lead to using downers again. This stage may be over in as little as six months, or it may last for the remainder of addicts' lives. The termination stage is the point at which temptation no longer exists and former addicts may consider the problem over. According to some experts, however, addiction never completely goes away. There is always that temptation to go back to using, which is why the only way to stay completely clean is never to try downers and other incredibly disgusting drugs.

Glossary

addiction The state in which a user is physically or psychologically dependent on a drug and feels compelled to keep taking it.

barbiturate A type of highly addictive depressant, once manufactured in many forms as popular sedatives and sleep aids.

benzodiazepine Any of a number of depressants manufactured as sedatives or tranquilizers.

depressants Drugs that suppress or reduce the activity of the central nervous system, producing calming or euphoric effects. The category includes barbiturates, benzodiazepines, opiates/opioids, and alcohol, all of which can be addictive.

hypnotic A depressant that induces sleep or a description of a sleeplike state.

sedative A depressant that produces feelings of calm and relaxation.

tolerance A characteristic of certain drugs in which the effects diminish with continued use so that the user has to take larger doses to achieve the desired effects.

tranquilizers Depressants used to reduce stress or tension.

withdrawal Symptoms that occur when a habitual drug user suddenly stops taking the drug.

Center for Substance Abuse Prevention
Parklawn Building, Room 12-105
5600 Fishers Lane
Rockville, MD 20857
(301) 443-8956
E-mail: info@samhsa.org
Web site: http://www.samhsa.gov/centers/csap/csap.html

Drug Enforcement Administration
2401 Jefferson Davis Highway
Alexandria, VA 22301
(202) 307-1000
Web site: http://www.dea.gov

Narcotics Anonymous
World Services Office
P.O. Box 9999
Van Nuys, CA 91409
(818) 773-9999
Web site: http://www.na.org

National Center on Addiction and Abuse
  at Columbia University

633 3rd Avenue, 19th Floor
New York, NY 10017-6706
(212) 841-5200
Web site: http://www.casacolumbia.org

National Institute on Drug Abuse

Neuroscience Center Building
6001 Executive Boulevard
Rockville, MD 20852
(301) 443-1124
E-mail: information@lists.nida.nih.gov
Web site: http://www.nida.nih.gov

Office of National Drug Control Policy

Drug Policy Information Clearinghouse
P.O. Box 6000
Rockville, MD 20849-6000
(800) 666-3332
Web site: http://www.ncjrs.org

The Partnership for a Drug-Free America

405 Lexington Avenue, Suite 1601
New York, NY 10174
(212) 922-1560
Web site: http://www.drugfree.org

Substance Abuse and Mental Health Administration
1 Choke Cherry Road
Rockville, MD 20857
Web site://www.samhsa.gov

Web Sites
Due to the changing nature of Internet links, Rosen Publishing has developed an online list of Web sites related to the subject of this book. This site is updated regularly. Please use this link to access the list:

http://www.rosenlinks.com/idd/doda

For Further Reading

Bayer, Linda. *Drugs, Crime, and Criminal Justice.* Philadelphia, PA: Chelsea House Publishers, 2001.

Egendorf, Laura K. *Chemical Dependency: Opposing Viewpoints.* Farmington Hills, MI: Greenhaven Press, 2003.

Houle, Michelle M. *Tranquilizer, Barbiturate, and Downer Drug Dangers.* Berkeley Heights, NJ: Enslow Publishers, Inc., 2000.

Hyde, Margaret O. *Drugs 101: An Overview for Teens.* Brookfield, CT: 21st Century, 2003.

Moreno, Tina, Bettie B. Youngs, and Jennifer Leigh Youngs. *A Teen's Guide to Living Drug-Free.* Deerfield Beach, FL: Health Communications, Inc., 2003.

Rodriguez, Joseph. *Juvenile.* New York, NY: powerHouse Books, 2004.

Ryan, Elizabeth A. *Straight Talk About Drugs and Alcohol.* New York, NY: Facts on File, 1996.

Bibliography

Emmett, David, and Graeme Nice. *Understanding Street Drugs: A Handbook of Substance Misuse for Parents, Teachers, and Other Professionals*. 2nd ed. Philadelphia, PA: Jessica Kingsley Publishers, 2006.

Gahlinger, Paul. *Illegal Drugs: A Complete Guide to Their History, Chemistry, Use, and Abuse*. New York, NY: Plume, 2004.

Julien, Robert M. *A Primer of Drug Action: A Concise, Nontechnical Guide to the Actions, Uses, and Side Effects of Psychoactive Drugs*. 8th ed. New York, NY: W. H. Freeman and Company, 2000.

Kuhn, Cynthia, et al. *Buzzed: The Straight Facts About the Most Used and Abused Drugs from Alcohol to Ecstasy*. 2nd ed. New York, NY: W. W. Norton and Company, 2003.

Kuhn, Cynthia, et al. *Just Say Know: Talking with Kids About Drugs and Alcohol*. New York, NY: W. W. Norton and Company, 2002.

Rudgley, Richard. *The Encyclopedia of Psychoactive Substances*. New York, NY: Thomas Dunne Books, 2000.

Somdahl, Gary L. *Drugs and Kids: How Parents Can Keep Them Apart*. Salem, OR: Dimi Press, 1996.

Index

About the Author

Jason Porterfield has written more than twenty books for Rosen Publishing. Porterfield graduated from Oberlin College in 2001, with majors in English, history, and religion. He currently lives in Chicago.

Photo Credits

Cover, p. 1 © www.istockphoto.com/ericsphotography; pp. 7, 33 © AP/ Wide World Photos; p. 9 Drug Enforcement Administration; p. 10 © Justin Sullivan/Getty Images; p. 13 © www.istockphoto.com/Clint Spencer; p. 15 © Amanda Edwards/Getty Images; p. 16 © www. istockphoto.com/ranplett; p. 19 © www.istockphoto.com/Aleksej Kostin; pp. 22, 28 © Custom Medical Stock Photo; p. 24 © Pascal Goetgheluck/Photo Researchers, Inc.; p. 27 © Jonathan Ferrey/Getty Images; p. 30 © Kairos, Latin Stock/Photo Researchers, Inc.; p. 34 © Scott Olson/Getty Images; pp. 37, 39 © Jordan Silverman/Getty Images.

Designer: Les Kanturek; **Editor:** Nicholas Croce
Photo Researcher: Amy Feinberg